MARGIT: BOOK THREE
OPEN YOUR
DOORS
KATHY KACER

**Look for the other Margit stories
in Our Canadian Girl**

MARGIT: BOOK THREE
OPEN YOUR DOORS
KATHY KACER

PENGUIN
CANADA

PENGUIN CANADA

Published by the Penguin Group

Penguin Group (Canada), 90 Eglinton Avenue East, Suite 700, Toronto, Ontario, Canada M4P 2Y3
(a division of Pearson Penguin Canada Inc.)

Penguin Group (USA) Inc., 375 Hudson Street, New York, New York 10014, U.S.A.
Penguin Books Ltd, 80 Strand, London WC2R 0RL, England
Penguin Ireland, 25 St Stephen's Green, Dublin 2, Ireland (a division of Penguin Books Ltd)
Penguin Group (Australia), 250 Camberwell Road, Camberwell, Victoria 3124, Australia
(a division of Pearson Australia Group Pty Ltd)
Penguin Books India Pvt Ltd, 11 Community Centre, Panchsheel Park, New Delhi – 110 017, India
Penguin Group (NZ), cnr Airborne and Rosedale Roads, Albany, Auckland 1310, New Zealand
(a division of Pearson New Zealand Ltd)
Penguin Books (South Africa) (Pty) Ltd, 24 Sturdee Avenue, Rosebank, Johannesburg 2196,
South Africa

Penguin Books Ltd, Registered Offices: 80 Strand, London WC2R 0RL, England

First published 2006

1 2 3 4 5 6 7 8 9 10 (WEB)

Copyright © Kathy Kacer, 2006
Illustrations © Janet Wilson, 2006
Design: Matthews Communications Design Inc.
Map copyright © Sharon Matthews

Manufactured in Canada.

LIBRARY AND ARCHIVES CANADA CATALOGUING IN PUBLICATION

Kacer, Kathy, 1954–
Margit : open your doors / Kathy Kacer.

(Our Canadian girl)
"Margit: Book Three".
ISBN 0-14-305009-5

1. Refugees, Jewish—Ontario—Toronto—Juvenile fiction.
I. Title. II. Title: Open your doors. III. Series.

PS8571.A33M39 2006   jC813'.54   C2005-905922-2

Visit the Penguin Group (Canada) website at **www.penguin.ca**

For Gabi and Jake,

with love as always

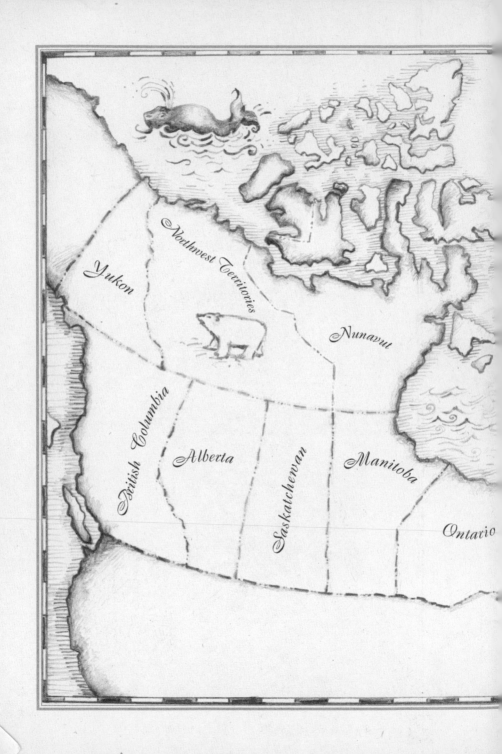

Canada

Newfoundland and Labrador

Quebec

P.E.I.

New Brunswick

Nova Scotia

 Marks the location of the story

MARGIT'S STORY CONTINUES

B Y THE TIME WORLD WAR II ENDS in 1945, more than 250 000 Jewish people in Europe have been left homeless. Among them are thousands of children whose parents have died or been killed at the hands of Adolf Hitler and his Nazi armies. These Jewish orphans have no families and no homes. Very few countries in the world are willing to admit these young survivors of the Holocaust.

Canada continues to maintain a strict immigration policy. The government, under Prime Minister Mackenzie King, is afraid that those who have survived Hitler's violence and who want to come to Canada might be a threat to Canadians and might take jobs away from Canadian citizens.

The Canadian Jewish community is trying desperately to convince the government to loosen its restrictions on Jewish refugees, but to no avail. In 1946, a woman by the name of Charity Grant joins the lobbying efforts of those trying to help Jewish refugees in Europe, especially the children. She is part of a Canadian team of the United Nations Relief and Rehabilitation Administration (UNRRA). She writes numerous letters to the prime minister, asking him to allow Canada to open its doors to European Jewish children who were orphaned during the war.

In 1947, the Canadian government finally issues Order in Council #1647 granting permission for one thousand Jewish war orphans to enter the country. Members of the Canadian Jewish Congress work with the UNRRA to find orphans under the age of eighteen and help them come to Canada.

Margit hears that Jewish orphans are about to be admitted to Canada. She remembers what it was like to come to a strange country and to feel all alone. She at least had her mother to protect her. Margit can't imagine what it would feel like to have no one. She wants to help and she has a plan. She wants one of the Jewish orphans to come and live with her family. But her parents are reluctant. They are just beginning to feel comfortable in Canada after a long struggle to adjust. How could they possibly take in another child?

Margit is determined to show that she is responsible and able to help take care of a new child. But will she be able to convince her parents to open their hearts and their doors to a Jewish orphan?

CHAPTER N° 1

Margit hugged her little brother closer to her chest before crossing the busy intersection. "Stop squirming, Jack," she pleaded anxiously as rush hour traffic whizzed by on the streets of downtown Toronto.

Jack did not make it easy. He twisted and wriggled in her arms. "Go down, Mah-git," he begged.

"I'll let you down in a minute—once we're in the market." It was impossible at times to manage her two-year-old brother. Jack could not keep still. Margit had to hold on to him every minute or he might disappear. The family called him their little wanderer. "If you're good, I'll get you a Popsicle when we get to Mr. Borofsky's store—I promise."

Jack stopped struggling and looked up at his sister. His round, impish face broke into a triumphant grin. The only thing that kept him still was the promise of a treat—and even that usually lasted only a few minutes. "I be good, Mah-git," promised Jack. It was as if he knew he had won this round.

His sister sighed. Mamma would not be pleased that Margit was bribing Jack with sweets—especially this close to dinner. But she had no choice. How else was she to control him? Sometimes it was just unfair that her mother expected her to watch her little brother.

"If not you, then who else can we count on for help?" her Papa always said.

Well, sometimes thirteen-year-old Margit Freed didn't want to be dependable. Sometimes she just wanted to be a young girl, to be with her friends and not have to worry about chores and responsibilities.

Margit turned the corner onto Baldwin Street and bent to put Jack down. She gripped his hand tightly in hers before he could dart off into the crowd. The streets of Kensington Market were crawling with shoppers jostling one another on the congested sidewalks. Next to Margit, the fishmonger reached into a big wooden barrel, held up a dripping fish, and shouted loudly, "Fat pickled herring!" Beside him, the fruit vendor carolled in harmony, "Fresh fruit. None but the best. I eat 'em myself." Ancient women with shawl-covered heads haggled over their purchases: "Three cukes for ten cents? Down the street I can get them for seven." Margit paused to get her bearings. *Let's see,* she thought to herself. *Mamma needs sugar and flour from the dry goods store, and bread from the bakery.*

"Popsicle," cried Jack, tugging persistently on Margit's arm.

Margit groaned. She should have brought the carriage. But Jack hated being confined in his buggy even more than being held. Besides,

Margit thought the trip would be quicker this way. She was beginning to realize she was wrong.

"I thought you had so much homework to do." Margit looked up to see Alice approaching from a nearby shop. Margit brightened at the sight of her best friend. Margit had met Alice almost two years earlier in practically this very spot, the day after Margit had arrived from her home country of Czechoslovakia. Since then, so much had happened to Margit. She had struggled with English, attended school, and learned the customs of Canadians. There had been ups and downs, but the one thing that had remained constant and true was her friendship with Alice.

"I do have homework—and lots of it," Margit replied, brushing her curly brown hair off her shoulders. "But I had to help my mother with some errands. And I'm in charge of Jack as well."

Alice bent to greet Jack. "Hi, there," she said, playfully poking Jack's tummy. "Do you want to come into my parents' flower shop?"

"Popsicle," Jack replied, looking up again at Margit.

"I'm having trouble handling him," said Margit. "I didn't want to bring him, but my mother insisted. She had to finish some sewing for the tailor and Jack was being impossible—like he is right now."

Jack tugged and pulled on Margit's arm. "Popsicle," he insisted, louder this time. "Popsicle, Mah-git!"

"What am I going to do?" Margit asked.

"He's so cute," laughed Alice, "and funny."

"That's easy for you to say. You don't have a baby brother to watch." Silently, Margit blamed her mother once more for making her look after Jack.

"Come on," said Alice. "I'll help you with Jack so you can get the things for your mother. Then, we'll all get a Popsicle, right, Jack?"

"Popsicle," Jack replied, for what seemed like the hundredth time.

Alice laughed and ducked into her parents' store, under the sign that read "Donald's Flowers."

She emerged a moment later. Mrs. Donald waved to Margit from inside the shop as the girls moved off, swinging Jack through the air between them.

With Alice's help, Margit quickly finished her shopping and carefully counted the change from the money her mother had given her. There was just enough left over for two Popsicles, one for Jack and one for Margit and Alice to share. The girls settled on a curb outside the sweet shop with Jack in between them, happily slurping on his prize. Even though it was late afternoon, the spring sun was still warm in the sky. Margit loved this time of year. It wasn't yet sweltering hot, like it would be in July and August. But it was warm enough to be outside without a jacket, and the days were slowly lengthening. They still had hours before the sun would set.

"So, what homework do you have?" asked Alice as a big truck rumbled down the street. It stopped in front of the fruit stall, blocking the traffic in both directions. Car horns blasted and motorists yelled.

Margit gasped. "Thanks for reminding me," she said, pulling Jack to his feet. "I've got to get home. My parents are making me go to this meeting at the synagogue tonight. And I probably have to help with the dinner dishes before we go, and who knows what else they're going to make me do. I'm never going to get to my homework."

"Stop complaining, Margit," replied Alice. "You act like you're the only one with chores. I work in my parents' flower shop almost every day after school—homework or not."

"But at least your parents pay you for the work. That's fair. Watching Jack every day isn't." Margit knew her argument was weak. Everyone had responsibilities. She understood that. But sometimes hers felt overwhelming.

Alice stood and shrugged her shoulders. "Like I said, we all have things to do."

CHAPTER N° 2

"Stop fidgeting, Margit," Mamma whispered sharply as she turned to stare at her daughter.

Margit looked up at her mother blankly. She had been lost in her own thoughts and shook her head slightly, as if to focus. "It's late, Mamma," she whispered back. "I need to get home so I can finish my homework."

Margit, along with her mother, her father, and Jack, were seated in the large hall of their synagogue. The hall was packed with families, all gathered to listen to the guest speaker. Margit had not wanted to come.

"I've got too much to do tonight," she had complained after returning from the market with Jack. "You're the ones who keep telling me I've got to work hard. And now you want me to give up an evening to go to the synagogue and listen to some boring person talk." Margit thought back over the past year and the struggles she sometimes had in school. She worked hard. No one could doubt that. And in some subjects, Margit was at the top of her class. But other subjects, like science, were still a struggle. Margit couldn't believe that her parents actually wanted her to go out on a school night.

"This is important," Papa said. "A woman from the United Nations is coming to talk about the war and what it has done to our people—Jewish families like us who lost everything."

In the end, there wasn't much Margit could do. Besides, Papa looked so eager to hear this speaker. And who could blame him? He was one of the lucky ones who had survived the war and come to Canada in 1946 to join his family.

9

Millions of others had not been so lucky. Margit was thankful every day of her life that her family was together and living in Toronto. Still, sometimes she wished that they would just forget about the awful war now that it was over. It seemed so long ago in Margit's young mind. Her thoughts were on the life she had now—her friends and her school.

Margit groaned softly. *When will this meeting end?* she wondered as she sat up in her seat and looked around. Mamma glanced again at her daughter, motioning once more for her to sit still. It was bad enough that Jack had a hard time staying in one place. Everyone expected the baby of the family to be distracted, but they did not expect it of Margit.

Suddenly, the room quieted as the rabbi made his way to the lectern. He adjusted the microphone and cleared his throat.

"My friends," he began. "Thank you for coming out tonight. I know you are all busy with your lives and it is difficult to come together. But I am grateful you are here."

Please let this evening end soon, prayed Margit as she settled to hear what the rabbi had to say.

"Almost two years have passed since the end of the terrible war that took the lives of more than six million of our brothers and sisters in Europe. Here in our own synagogue, we have members who were lucky to survive and who have since joined our community."

Margit squirmed again as people in the synagogue turned toward her family.

"It is my honour to introduce a woman who will talk to us tonight about the plight of some young people who are still suffering, despite the end of the war. I will let her explain her story. Please join me in welcoming Miss Charity Grant."

The audience responded with warm applause as a young woman rose to stand behind the lectern. She adjusted her dark glasses, pushed her short brown hair off her forehead, and began to speak.

"Thank you, Rabbi, for allowing me to speak here tonight. In the past year, I've been travelling to communities across the country. I want to tell you about the work that I have been doing to save the Jewish children who were left behind in Europe after the end of the war. Their parents all died at the hands of Adolf Hitler and his evil Nazi followers. Many of these children suffered as well." Charity Grant paused and gazed out at the congregation. The audience was silent and attentive to her every word.

"I don't know how to describe what I feel about my mission. I am committed to saving lives, especially the lives of children. It's no secret that it has taken Canada and other countries a long time to allow refugees—those who managed to survive Hitler's slaughter—to enter our country. Even now, though things are much improved, it is still difficult to get into Canada if you are a survivor of the war."

Mamma and Papa nodded. It had been an almost impossible task to bring Papa into Canada after the war. Had it not been for Mamma's persistence, and the help of the Jewish Immigrant

Aid Society in Toronto, he may never have been allowed in. Margit sat up, curious now about what Miss Grant would have to say.

"Let me read from a letter that I wrote to Prime Minister Mackenzie King's government in January 1946: 'I wish Canada would offer to take a group of Jewish children. So far, no country has offered any permanent haven to any of them. Canada says it must play the part of a major power. Well let her show herself. Let her be the first to offer refuge to some of these children.'"

Charity Grant looked up from the letter she was reading to face her audience once more. She smiled. "I am here to tell you that Canada has finally responded. The government has agreed to allow one thousand Jewish orphans of the Holocaust to enter Canada."

The synagogue buzzed with excited chatter. Charity Grant raised her arms, trying to quiet the audience.

"I'm so pleased to hear your excitement. I take it that you are happy with the outcome of my

13

work." The congregation responded with warm applause. "Good! Because we will certainly need your generosity in the months to come. Anything you can do to open your doors to these young survivors will be greatly appreciated. Let me tell you how you can help."

Charity Grant continued talking for a few more minutes, but Margit had stopped listening. Who were these children? Where did they come from? How old were they? And even when they did come to Canada, where would they stay once they were here? Margit's homework was suddenly forgotten as her head filled with these and other questions. She needed to think. She needed to talk to her parents, maybe even talk to Charity Grant. But there was no time. The evening had ended. Margit's parents were heading out the door and calling for her to follow.

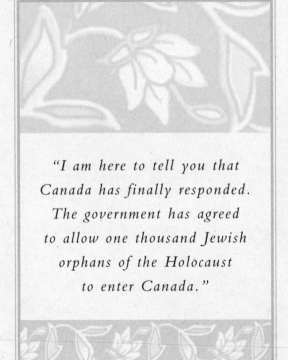

*"I am here to tell you that
Canada has finally responded.
The government has agreed
to allow one thousand Jewish
orphans of the Holocaust
to enter Canada."*

CHAPTER № 3

Margit was quiet on the walk home. She followed her parents as they wound their way through the dark streets of Toronto. The night-time air was cool and refreshing. But there was a feeling that the heat of summer was just around the corner, and everything was in readiness for its arrival. Margit caught a whiff of the fragrance of budding flowers in the air. It was mixed with the familiar smells of the city as her family passed through the streets of Kensington Market, close to their home. The fishmonger was closing up his stall, shovelling ice into buckets that would be dumped into the sewers. Here and there, older women sat on their front stoops, watching the people walk by and fanning themselves, almost anticipating summer, when the nights would be sweltering long after the sun went down. Up ahead, Jack slept heavily on his father's shoulder.

"It's a miracle that children have survived the war," said Mamma, as Margit listened in on her parents' conversation. They spoke in rapid Czech, the language of their home country. Margit had no difficulty following the conversation. Even though she now spoke English like one who had been born here, she still spoke mostly Czech with her parents. Their English had improved, but it was still difficult for them.

"And a blessing that Canada will provide a home for some of them," agreed Papa.

"The Jewish centres and group homes will need so many things for these children," continued Mamma. "I'll gather some clothes that Margit has outgrown."

Papa nodded. "They say that the children who are coming are between the ages of eight and eighteen. So, some of Margit's things will be perfect. Maybe even my old jackets for the older boys."

"I'll try to make some new clothes—in the evenings, when I've finished my work for the tailor."

The conversation continued as Margit kept pace a few steps behind her parents. Her mind was still spinning with the news of the arrival of the Jewish orphans. *What would it be like to be an orphan?* she wondered. What would it be like to be without your parents, without people who loved you and took care of you? It had been hard enough for Margit to come to Canada without Papa. In those early days, when she had wondered and worried about her father's whereabouts, at least she had had her mother to comfort her.

How did these children survive the terrible war? Were they hurt? Sometimes, even still, Papa would cry out at night. It was as if the memories of his experiences in the war had wounded him so deeply that the pain was still there, emerging in the dark night when everything else was quiet. Had these children also been in concentration camps—the prisons where so many Jews had been tortured and killed? Yes, it was a good thing that they were coming to live in Canada. But was that enough? Canada was only a country. It wasn't a mother or a father or a sibling or an aunt. It wasn't family. It was just a place. Margit felt in her heart that these children needed more. And already she had an idea of what she needed to do.

As soon as they entered the apartment, Margit turned to her parents, nearly bursting with excitement. "I have an idea," she began. "I think we should bring one of the orphans to live with us here." There! She had said it, the idea that had been percolating in her mind since Charity Grant's announcement in the synagogue earlier that evening. "That woman, Miss Grant, said that the orphans needed our help. This is the best kind of help we can offer—a home for one of them." Margit's voice trailed off as she stared at the startled faces of her Mamma and Papa. Mamma spoke first.

"I need to put this sleeping boy to bed," she said, reaching to lift Jack off Papa's shoulder. "Margit, make some tea for your papa and we'll talk in a moment."

Margit opened her mouth to speak, but the look on her mother's face stopped her. She moved to the kitchen to boil the water for tea. By the time Mamma joined them, Margit and her Papa were seated silently at the table, each cupping a steaming glass of tea with lemon. Papa stirred some sugar into the glass before looking at his daughter.

"Your heart is so big and kind, Margitka," he said, using her special nickname. "But this idea of yours is out of the question."

"How could we possibly manage to house another child?" Mamma added. "First of all, there is barely enough space in this apartment for the four of us."

It was true. The apartment was small—only one bedroom, one bathroom, a living room, and a kitchen. Jack still slept with Mamma and Papa in a crib in their bedroom. Margit's room was a curtained-off area in the living room. It offered some privacy and Margit loved the space. But where would another child fit?

"I've already thought of that," replied Margit eagerly. "We could put a rollaway bed in the living room. I'll even sleep there and give the girl my bedroom." Already this orphan had become a girl. Margit could almost envision her, this child who was becoming a member of the family even though she didn't yet exist.

"Even if we had the space," continued Mamma, "that's only one issue."

"We are barely keeping our own heads above water," said Papa. "And now, to take in another child. That is a huge responsibility. You don't know what you are asking, Margit."

"But you yourself have said that your job is getting so much better, Papa," argued Margit. "Mr. Hillock has handed over more and more work to you. He's even talked about a partnership." Papa worked at Hillock's Lumberyard as an accountant. Papa had worked hard and had earned the trust and respect of his boss. Even though Papa had had to give up his law practice when he came to Canada, he was proud of the work that he did at the lumberyard.

"Yes," agreed Papa. "And all of that means that we can live in some comfort. Perhaps your mamma won't have to count every penny any more. Maybe Jack can have some new toys and not just the ones that are bought second-hand. You could get some new things."

"I don't want new things," argued Margit. "I'll gladly give up new things if it means we can help an orphan child."

Back and forth, the argument continued, with no resolution. Margit and her parents each held firmly to their positions. Finally, Papa stood up from the table and looked at his watch. "It's enough for tonight," he said wearily. "We must all get some sleep."

"But—" began Margit.

"No," Mamma continued. "Your papa said it's enough and he's right. You still have homework, Margit. Do it quickly and go to sleep." Mamma and Papa turned their backs on their daughter and closed the door to their bedroom. Margit could still hear them talking to each other as she moved behind the curtain to her bed. Quickly, she finished her homework, rushing through the assignments in geography and math. Margit didn't care how she completed the work tonight. There were more important thoughts swirling in her head. By the time she climbed into bed, Margit's mind was racing.

She knew about persistence—about going after something she wanted. Hadn't she gotten that part in the school play earlier in the year when no one thought she could? Other girls were expected to get the starring roles. But

Margit had worked in secret, practising and memorizing the lines, and trying to imagine herself as the character. On the day of the audition, Margit's performance stood out above all others. Her parents actually cried the night they came to see her in the show. Yes, Margit knew how to get things that were important to her. And having an orphan child come to live with her family felt like her most important mission yet. Her campaign to adopt a Jewish orphan had just begun, and she would not let up until she had won.

CHAPTER N°4

Margit rubbed her puffy eyes, trying desperately to wipe the weariness away. She had barely slept. This morning, Margit's eyelids felt as heavy as lead, but her head was still spinning with dreams and ideas about having a Jewish orphan come and live with her family.

At the front of the classroom, Mrs. Cook's voice droned on and on, something about light sources and a lesson on energy. Margit could not listen. She stared at the clock above the door, watching the seconds tick by. Would the morning ever end? When the recess bell finally rang, Margit flew out the door, dragging Alice behind her.

"What is wrong with you?" demanded Alice, as the girls made their way to their favourite bench in the busy playground. "You looked like a zombie in class, and now you're so wound up, I can hardly keep up with you."

"We need to talk," replied Margit, pulling her friend down to sit next to her. Excitedly, Margit began to tell Alice about her idea. She described the evening before at the synagogue and Charity Grant's lecture. She talked about the plight of the orphaned Jewish children and how they needed help. She described the Canadian government's decision to allow one thousand orphans to enter Canada. Finally, she told Alice about her plan to have one child come and live with her family.

When she was finished, Margit sat back, waiting for her friend's reaction. Alice's face slowly broke into an enthusiastic smile. "That's great, Margit!" she said at last. "It's fantastic that your family is so willing to take in a child. I mean, it's so generous. But I'm not surprised. Your parents are the kindest people I know. Of course, they'd want to help...." Alice's voice trailed off as she saw Margit begin to frown. "What's wrong? Is there something I've missed?"

Margit paused. "Well, there is one problem. You see, this is *my* plan, not my parents'. They don't think we can take anyone in. That's why I need to talk to you. You've got to help me convince them that this is the right thing to do, the only thing to do. Somehow they have to see how much I want this."

Alice shook her head. "I don't know, Margit. I think your idea is great, but this is such a big responsibility. You complain when you have to do the dishes or when you have to watch Jack. I'm not sure I understand why you want someone to come and live with you, especially when your parents are against it."

Margit paused, trying to put her thoughts together. How could she explain to Alice what this meant to her, why it was so important? She was still having trouble understanding it herself.

Finally, Margit looked over at her friend and began to talk. "When my mother and I were trying to escape from Europe, it felt like no one would be able to save us. Then when we got here, it was still so hard. Sometimes, I felt so alone, even though I met you and I had my mother. I'm trying to understand what these orphans must feel like. And it isn't enough just to collect clothes for them or donate toys and books. I've tried talking to my parents, tried to explain all of this to them. But they just won't listen."

Alice eyed her friend thoughtfully. "I'm not sure this is the kind of thing you're going to be able to talk your parents into doing."

Margit shook her head. "Do you remember last year when you wanted that puppy, and your parents said no?" Alice had set out on a quest to talk her parents into buying her a dog. She spent months researching the type of dog that she wanted. She cut out photographs of puppies from magazines and borrowed books from the library. She left articles for her parents about the benefits of having a family pet, saved her allowance to help with the expenses, and did her chores without reminder. "Well, all of your work paid off, didn't it?" asked Margit.

Alice nodded. "Yes, and Ginger is the best dog I could ever have. But don't you see, Margit? That's just a dog! You're talking about convincing your parents to bring home a person. It's not the same thing."

Margit had stopped listening. There was something about what she had just said to Alice that gave her an idea, a sudden inspiration. "You know, Alice? Maybe the two things aren't so different after all. I know a dog and a person are not the same thing. But maybe I have to think of this project just the same way you thought about getting a pet. I'm not going to *talk* my parents into this. But I am going to find a way to *show* them it's the right thing to do. Come on," she said as the bell rang to signal the end of recess. "Will you come to the library with me after school? I've got work to do, and I need your help."

CHAPTER N<u>o</u> 5

Margit and Alice walked up the steep steps of the Central Reference Library. "Excuse me," Margit said politely to the lady seated at the front desk. "My friend and I are looking for some recent newspapers." Margit quickly explained about the information she was seeking and she and Alice were directed to the Reading Room.

"You'll find everything you're looking for at the back," the lady said, pointing over her shoulder. "The newspapers are sorted by name and date."

The tapping of Margit's shoes echoed up to the high ceiling as she and Alice walked across the Reading Room. Margit raised herself on her tiptoes to hush the sound. The room could hold two hundred and fifty people. On this afternoon, only about fifty people were there, spread out at the long rectangular tables that filled the impressive hall, reading silently from books and magazines.

Margit and Alice selected several newspapers and moved to sit at one of the empty tables. They spread their selection of papers across the table and started to look through them. In newspapers across the country, there were reports of the one thousand Jewish children who were to enter Canada. Each paper had facts about the government's decision, how it had been reached, and who was responsible.

"Here," whispered Margit. "Look at this." She pointed to an article from the *Victoria Daily Times*. Its headline proclaimed, "1000 JEWISH CHILDREN, ORPHANED BY NAZIS, TO GET HOMES IN CANADA."

The article went on to explain that there were thousands of children scattered across Europe

"Here," whispered Margit.
"Look at this."

who were in need of sanctuary and that Canada had an obligation to help them. Margit copied some of the information into her notebook and then looked up. "This is important," she said. "I need to show my parents that bringing these orphans to Canada is something that the whole country knows about. It's not just our synagogue or a couple of people who are concerned. It's more important than that." She shook her head in some frustration. "But this isn't enough. This isn't the kind of information that will budge my parents or make them want to bring a child into our own home."

Alice was busy poring over another newspaper. Suddenly, she looked up, her eyes bright and filled with enthusiasm. "You want something that will move your parents? Well, I think I've found it. Read this."

She passed the article over to Margit, who quickly read through it. By the time she was finished, her whole body was tingling with excitement and energy. "It's perfect!" Margit cried and then quickly looked around, startled at the sound of her voice in the great hall. She and Alice giggled quietly. Then, Margit stood up from the table, taking the article with her. She approached the main desk and whispered once more to the lady in charge. Alice watched and held her breath as the lady nodded silently, folded the paper in half, placed it in a large envelope, and gave it back to Margit.

"We usually don't lend the newspapers," the woman said. "But in this case, I'll make an exception. Bring it back next week," she added.

"Oh, thank you," Margit cried enthusiastically. She grabbed Alice's arm and the two girls bolted out the door of the library.

By the time Margit arrived home, Mamma was busy preparing supper. "Margit! Finally, you're home. I was beginning to worry," Mamma said as Margit entered the apartment and placed her schoolbag on a chair.

"Sorry, Mamma," Margit replied. "I, uh, had to talk to my teacher after class."

"Talk to the teacher? Are you having problems? Something you aren't telling me?"

"No, Mamma. Everything's fine. I promise. Here, let me help you." Margit grabbed an apron from a drawer and busied herself in the kitchen. First, she placed a large pot of water on the stove to boil, and then she reached for four potatoes from a bag next to the cupboard. She peeled and cut the potatoes with the skill of someone who had been helping in the kitchen for a long time. Next, Margit took plates and cutlery from the cabinet and moved over to set the table, adding glasses and napkins to finish. She was determined to show Mamma how cooperative she was and how delighted she was to be helping around the house. There would be no more complaining on her part, no more grumbling about too much responsibility.

"If you'd like, I'll watch Jack for you, Mamma," Margit said as the steam from the boiling water filled the small kitchen. "You've probably got some extra sewing to do. I'll keep an eye on him."

Jack was busy running around the kitchen table, dragging several pots stacked together behind him. They bounced off the floor and chairs, clanking loudly with a racket that ricocheted throughout the apartment. "Choo, choo," cried Jack, pretending to be the engine of a long line of small railway cars.

Mamma glanced up in surprise. It was unlike Margit to volunteer this help. "Yes," Mamma said. "Oh, thank you, Margit. I need your help so much. Jack is a handful."

Margit smiled enthusiastically and reached for her young brother. "Come on, Jack. Come play in my room. We'll let Mamma get some work done." Margit picked up her schoolbag from the chair and led Jack around the curtain into her private space. He loved going into this hideaway and giggled as Margit tossed him playfully onto her bed. "You stay with me, Jack," Margit said. "And don't bother Mamma. It's all part of the plan," she added quietly. "I'll show her we can manage another child. But you're going to have to help me, Jack." She stared at her baby brother. "You've got to cooperate and not cause any trouble. Can you do that? Can you be good?"

Jack gazed back at his big sister, cocking his head to one side and wrinkling his tiny brow. "I good, Mah-git," he replied almost knowingly.

Margit laughed and after a moment, Jack joined in.

Papa arrived home at seven o'clock, looking tired from his long day. As soon as she heard his key in the lock, Margit bounded for the door, eager to greet her father. "Here, Papa," she cried, taking his briefcase. "Let me hang up your coat. Would you like some tea before supper?"

Papa kissed his daughter lovingly on the forehead. "Ah, my Margitka. You are the best cure for my weariness."

"Papa!" cried Jack, plunging headlong at his father. He clutched Papa's pant leg, jumping up and down joyously.

"And how is my Jumping Jack?" Papa said, reaching down to pick up his son. Jack's little body twitched and shook with excitement as he grabbed his father's face and squeezed his cheeks. "It is a pleasure to come home to my family," Papa added, kissing Mamma, who was still bent over the sewing machine. "No tea for now, Margit," he added. "I smell a delicious supper and I am a hungry man."

"Come to the table," said Margit. "Supper's ready. I've helped prepare everything tonight. And I've even done most of my homework so I can do the dishes later if you want. You and Mamma can relax when supper's done." The family moved to sit down at the kitchen table.

"You should have seen Margit, Leo," Mamma said. "She cooked and she watched Jack, and all this with no complaint. Today, she was my star helper."

Papa looked delighted and he said, "You see, Miriam? I've always told you how responsible Margit can be. And now she's proving it. We can rely on her for anything."

Margit quickly brought the potatoes, cucumber salad, and meat goulash to the table. Mamma's stew was delicious: tender beef, simmered with carrots and sweet potatoes. Margit beamed. *All is going well,* she thought, as she passed the platters of food to her parents and took a helping for herself. As the family began to eat their meal, Margit leaned forward and looked at Mamma.

"I thought this Saturday that I would take Jack out for a few hours. I thought I would take him to the department store—to Eaton's and then maybe to the park. That way he'd be out of your hair. Alice said she'd come with me to help."

Mamma smiled back. "That would be wonderful, Margit. I could use some time here alone. Jack gets into everything in the apartment. It's impossible to get anything else done when I'm with him."

Margit nodded. "Maybe you and Papa could even go for a walk. You never have enough time to be together alone."

Papa reached for Margit's hand. "Our daughter is growing up, Miriam," he said. "She's a gem," he added. "A treasure, yes? She makes our lives a blessing and a pleasure. I am a rich man with this family of mine."

Margit had been waiting for this moment. Without hesitation, she turned to her parents and began to speak. "We need to talk about the Jewish orphans again," Margit began.

"Yes, I've been thinking more and more about this," said Papa. "Perhaps we can give some money after all. You were right, Margit, when you said my work was getting better. We have to give all we can when others are still suffering."

"That's great, Papa. But it's not enough. I still think we need to bring one of the children here to live with us. That's the best kind of help we can give."

Papa shook his head. "I told you before. It's out of the question. Helping with money and clothing is one thing. Bringing a child to live here is far too much for us to manage."

"But you see how I can help," protested Margit. "Like tonight—helping with meals and tidying, and even with Jack. I didn't complain, and I would do even more if we brought an orphan to live with us."

"Tonight you were a wonderful help, Margit. And as I said, it's what we expect you to do— what we rely on you for. But you can't spend all your time looking after the apartment. You're still a child yourself."

"How can you say that, Mamma?" Margit cried. "I'm more capable than anyone my age." Margit felt a flash of hot anger rise in her cheeks, and she worked hard to control her trembling voice. "I want you to see something that I read in one of the newspapers."

Without giving her parents a moment to reply, Margit left the table and ran to her bed. She opened her schoolbag and carefully pulled out the newspaper she had brought home from the library. "Before you say anything else, just listen to this," she said as she returned to sit at the table. "It's a bulletin from the Canadian Jewish Congress headquarters in Montreal." Margit began to read aloud from the article:

There is a Jewish child in Europe who is waiting for you to let him begin to live. He is the child for whom your heart bled when you read the news of Nazi violence a few years back. Today, he stands at your very doorstep, needing a home, a family, the love and guidance of a father and mother. You want to help this child, from the bottom of your heart. Is there room in your home for him—a place in the warmth of your family circle for which his heart is so hungry?

Margit finished reading and looked up at her parents. Mamma's eyes were filled with tears, and Papa's head hung low on his chest.

"My heart breaks for these children," Mamma whispered at last. "But there is nothing more we can do to help."

"But, Mamma," said Margit weakly, "how can we turn our backs on them?"

"We will help in the ways that we are able," said Papa with finality. "Now, Margit, do the dishes as you promised."

With that, he and Mamma rose from the table, taking Jack with them. Margit sat still. She was drained from the fight. She had used every argument she could think of, and she felt the world caving in on her. Her hopes for an orphan child were fading. Margit picked up the dishes and sadly moved to the sink.

CHAPTER № 7

For the next two days, Margit walked around in a glum cloud of sadness. Nothing interested her and nothing excited her. She moved through the activities of school and home like one of Jack's windup soldiers, marching stiffly through each day and then sitting motionless in the evening until it was time to start again the next morning. She took to answering her parents in one-word sentences, no matter how much they tried to engage her.

"How was school, today?" Papa would say with great enthusiasm.

"Fine," Margit replied.

"What special things did you do?"

"Nothing," she said.

Papa would try again and again to get his daughter to talk, to no avail. Finally, he would shake his head and turn away.

On Wednesday, Alice came home after school with Margit. Margit barely acknowledged her mother as the two girls entered the apartment.

"How nice I see you, Alice!" Mamma said warmly in her accented English. "Your parents good?"

"Hello, Mrs. Freed," Alice replied. "They're fine, thank you. They send their regards to—"

"We're going into my room, Mamma. We've got work to do," interrupted Margit.

"Yes, but maybe girls would like to sit with me and have a small snack. I make poppy-seed cake. Alice, I know you love my cake."

"No," replied Margit before Alice could respond. "We just want to go to my room.

Alone," she added before steering Alice quickly around the curtain.

"Did you see your mother's face?" Alice asked as the girls settled on Margit's bed. "She looked so hurt."

"I don't care," responded Margit. "They don't seem to mind how I feel. And I don't care about them."

Alice regarded her friend thoughtfully. "Stop pouting, Margit. And stop moping around like this. So you tried something and it didn't work. I understand that bringing an orphan to live with you was very important. But now you're treating your parents like they're terrible people."

Margit couldn't answer. She didn't want to think about what she might be doing to her parents. She could only think about what they had done to her. Her parents had ruined her plan, and she could not see it any other way. She dug into her schoolbag and pulled out her notebook to end the conversation with Alice. Alice shrugged her shoulders and the two girls began to work together on their homework. About an hour had passed when Margit's mother entered the bedroom, a tray of poppy-seed cake in her hands.

"You're too busy to sit with me, but I know Alice will enjoy this," she said looking around for a place to put the tray. "Besides, I know Alice will help you take Jack out on Saturday. So with my cake, I thank you."

Margit closed her eyes and sighed deeply. She had forgotten about her offer to help with Jack. Right now, it was the last thing she wanted to do.

"Margit, your room is a mess," Mamma exclaimed as she pushed aside some dirty cups and placed the tray down on the desk. "This is not like you. Why I have to remind you to tidy things?"

In the preceding days, Margit had stopped bothering about her room. Clothes were scattered on the floor and desk chair. Her bed was unmade and papers and books were piled high on her shelf. Mamma was right. It was unlike Margit to leave her room in such a state. But it was one more reminder that Margit had suddenly stopped caring about such things.

"I'll do it," replied Margit. "Later. Can't you see I'm busy now?"

"No," replied Mamma, bending to pick up Margit's skirt from the floor. When she spoke again, it was in Czech. "I've heard *later* too many times. I'm trying to be patient with you, Margit. But as soon as Alice leaves, I want you to clean your room. Immediately!" Mamma turned her back on her daughter and flung the curtain aside.

"Thank you for the cake," called Alice, looking helplessly after Margit's mother. Margit's face flamed, but she stared unmoving at the curtain.

"Maybe I should go, now," Alice said after several tense minutes had passed. "I'm sorry, Margit. But I can't be here any more. I'll see you tomorrow at school." Alice collected her things and said a quick goodbye to Margit's mother, leaving Margit alone on her bed.

Do this and do that, Margit thought angrily. *I don't care about anything any more. I don't want to help anyone.*

Jack suddenly poked his head around the curtain, wanting to play with his older sister. Margit was not in the mood.

"Get out, Jack," Margit shouted. "Can't you see I'm busy?"

"Play, Mah-git," Jack insisted, stamping his foot on the floor.

"I don't have any time to play with you. Leave me alone. Everybody, just leave me alone!" Jack's face crumpled and tears welled up in his eyes. He ran from the room sobbing and shouting for his mother.

"Tell Jack to stop bothering me, Mamma," said Margit following her brother into the living room.

"He doesn't understand, Margit," said Mamma, scooping up Jack and holding him closely, trying to comfort her sad little boy. "And frankly, neither do I. You've been angry and distant for days. What has gotten into you?"

"Nothing. Stop asking questions. Stop asking me to do things."

"I'm your mother," replied Mamma with calm authority. "I have a right to talk to you." Mamma took several deep breaths. "Margit, I'm trying to understand that you are upset about the orphans. But your behaviour is not helping anyone. And you are pushing me to the limit of my understanding."

Margit turned away, not wanting her mother to see the tears streaming down her cheeks. She stomped angrily into her room and threw herself onto her bed, pounding her pillow and burying her face in her feather comforter. No one understood her, not her parents and not even Alice. Margit had tried everything to convince her parents to bring a Jewish orphan into their home, and she had failed. Now, everyone expected her to act as if everything were fine. Well, it wasn't and she couldn't pretend it was. Was she being childish to be so angry with her parents? Was she feeling too sorry for herself? Even Alice thought she had gone too far. Well, Margit didn't think so.

By the time the weekend arrived, Margit had reached an uneasy truce with her parents. There were no formal apologies, just a slow but steady return to a more peaceful state. The morning after Alice's visit, Margit washed the breakfast dishes without being asked and tidied her room. Mamma packed Margit's favourite lunch of sliced salami on dark rye bread, with lots of mustard. And the next day, a book that Papa bought from a second-hand store appeared on Margit's shelf. It was called *Kathie's Three Wishes,* written by Amanda Douglas. Margit opened the book and read the first lines: "'0 DEAR!' and Kathie Alston closed her book with a sigh; 'if there were only real fairies! If one could wish for a thing and have it!'"

Margit still wished desperately that an orphan child could come and live with her family. Nothing could stop that longing. And in her heart, Margit knew that she wouldn't give up trying somehow to convince her parents to do it. But the truth was, Margit couldn't stay angry with her parents for too long, nor they with her.

Saturday morning arrived, and Margit awoke to a warm, sunny day. She dressed quickly, ate breakfast, and prepared Jack for their outing.

"I think you should take the carriage," Mamma said with some concern. "You'll be gone a long time and you know how hard it is to handle Jack."

"Don't worry, Mamma. Alice and I will hold onto Jack every second," replied Margit. "He hates being in the buggy."

"No baby," said Jack firmly, weighing in on the conversation. He pointed at the carriage in the corner of the living room. "I walk, Mah-git."

"There, you see? That settles it, Mamma," said Margit. "You're not a baby, Jack. You're going to walk, just like a big boy."

"No baby. I walk," nodded Jack triumphantly.

Mamma was still not convinced. "You must never let go of his hand," she insisted. Margit nodded. "And pick him up to cross the street."

"I will, Mamma."

"And—"

"Goodbye, Mamma." Margit kissed her mother on the cheek and opened the apartment door. "You and Papa have a wonderful day, and we'll see you later."

Margit was gone before Mamma could say anything else. Alice was already waiting on the sidewalk in front of Margit's small, brick building.

"I thought I'd never get out of there," said Margit as she greeted her friend. "Let's go, Jack."

Margit and Alice set out in the direction of College Street, laughing and talking easily, all the while carefully clutching Jack's chubby hands.

Despite his protests, Margit carried him across the busy street, as she had promised her mother. They boarded the streetcar that would take the three of them to Eaton's College Street store. They entered the store from Yonge Street, passing under the enormous Roman arch at the entrance.

Visiting the Eaton's department store was always a treat for Margit. It was almost like walking through an amusement park; there was so much to see and do. The children moved past glass counters filled with colourful silk scarves, and they smelled the fancy perfumes. They passed racks of fashionable hats and purses. People surged in all directions. Sales ladies beckoned their customers to their counters. Margit stumbled after Alice, still clutching Jack's hand. It was as if she couldn't walk and see everything at the same time. She tried to take it all in, her eyes moving in ever-growing circles as they all headed for the elevator. Up they rode, until the doors to the elevator opened on the fourth floor and Margit, Alice, and Jack stepped out into a magical world.

The toy department was a young person's paradise. Jack's mouth dropped open with delight and he bounced up and down shouting, "Boat! Car! Train!" All those toys and more were displayed on high shelves and wooden counters. There were books, dress-up clothes, and colourful crayons and paper, all beckoning the children to come forward and see, touch, and experience their wonder. There was one entire section of games. Margit passed by two boys engaged in a serious game of crokinole, each one flicking his wooden disks onto the eight-sided board, trying to get as close to the twenty-point centre as possible.

"Car!" insisted Jack, tugging hard on Margit's hand.

"Wait, Jack. Not yet," Margit replied. She reached into her pocket and pulled out a large lollipop. She had brought it from home, knowing that she might need it during the day for Jack. Now was the right moment to use it. "Here, Jack," said Margit, kneeling in front of her brother.

"Yum," shouted Jack as he grabbed the lollipop, pulled off its wrapper, and shoved the sweet treat into his mouth. Jack was content for the moment, and Margit stood up. She would get to the cars and trucks in a few minutes. But before that, she and Alice had to see the dolls.

There were dozens of them, mountains of dolls, in all shapes and sizes, stacked together on shelves, linking their arms and legs like pieces of a giant puzzle. Margit carefully selected a large lifelike doll and looked at the tag. Her name was Violet and she was part of a collection of dolls known as the Eaton's Beauties. Margit gazed at Violet's long brown ringlets and her porcelain face. She wore a pale blue lace dress and even carried a small purse in her hand. Meanwhile, Alice had picked up another doll in a white satin wedding gown with matching satin socks and dress slippers. Her name was Eva, and she had blond curly hair and the bluest eyes Margit had ever seen. Alice and Margit looked at each other and sighed longingly. Neither spoke. They didn't need to. It was enough just to hold these beautiful dolls and dream of owning one. For the next few minutes, Margit and Alice ran from doll to doll, naming each one aloud, admiring their clothes, and dancing with them in the aisles of the store. Everything else was forgotten.

Suddenly, Margit stopped in her tracks and looked around. "Where's Jack?" she asked.

CHAPTER N°9

"Where's Jack?" Margit asked again, this time louder.

Alice froze. "I thought you were holding him."

"I was, but I must have let go of his hand." Panic seized Margit's heart and she fought to control the rising fear. "Jack? Jack!" Her breathing was quick and shallow as she raced up and down the aisles of the toy department, shouting Jack's name. Where could he have gone? She had been watching him so carefully, holding him tightly. Then, she had turned her back and, in a split second, her baby brother had disappeared.

"You must never let go of his hand." Mamma's voice echoed in Margit's ears. How could she possibly have let go of Jack? In her own desire to play with the dolls, she had forgotten her responsibility to her brother. How could she have done something so careless? This was Margit's worst nightmare.

"Let's not panic." Alice appeared at Margit's side. "He must be here somewhere. He can't have gone far. You take the car and truck sections. Jack said he wanted to go and see those toys. I'll search in the games department. Between the two of us, we'll find him in no time." Alice was trying to be reassuring, but even she sounded uncertain and afraid. Margit nodded and set off, calling Jack's name, scanning every aisle and looking behind every shelf, counter, and display case. Minutes went by and still there was no sign of Jack.

"I think we need to call a security guard," said Alice when she and Margit finally met up at the elevator.

"And Mamma," added Margit in a whisper. "I'd better call Mamma."

When the elevator doors opened and her parents rushed onto the floor, Mamma's face was already tear-stained and stricken. Making the telephone call to them had been one of the most difficult tasks of Margit's young life. Papa had answered the call. When Margit blurted that Jack was missing, she could hear the instant fear in his voice even as he tried to maintain control. Now they barely acknowledged Margit except to ask her the same questions the security guards had already asked.

"When did you see him last?"

"How long has he been missing?"

"Were you holding his hand?"

"I just wanted to see the dolls," whispered Margit. "I just let go of him for a minute. I'm so sorry."

Security guards were already on the floor, searching everywhere, calling Jack's name. Salespeople had joined the search, along with customers who offered their help.

"My son gets lost here all the time," a kind-faced woman said. "And then, suddenly, he reappears. I'm sure your boy will do the same."

"He is so little," replied Papa in his broken English. "I thank you for help." The woman nodded and resumed her search.

More minutes passed and still there was no sign of Jack. "I think we're going to have to spread out to some other floors," the guard said as he called Margit's family together. "We've covered every inch of the toy department, but there's no sign of your son. Perhaps he got onto the elevator with a group of shoppers."

The elevator! The nightmare was getting worse by the minute. Margit held her head in her hands and tried to block out the image of baby Jack waddling onto the elevator and being deposited onto another floor in a surge of pushy shoppers. Was he crying? Was he shouting her name somewhere? Margit couldn't even begin to imagine that he might be hurt.

"If we don't find him within another half hour, we'll contact the police," the security guard added, checking his watch.

"The police!" Papa's reaction was painful. This was not a reassuring plan for Margit's father. Margit knew that his mind was flashing back to the war and his own capture by the Nazis in Czechoslovakia. Police to Papa meant arrests and cruelty.

In desperation, Margit's eyes swept across the toy department once more. "Where are you, Jack?" she pleaded in a half-whisper. "Please answer me."

And then, she saw something—a flutter, a tiny movement—coming from a curtain that was draped over a long table in one empty corner of the floor. Without saying a word, Margit walked toward the curtain, holding her breath. She bent over and pushed it aside, and there was Jack, sleeping peacefully. His face was covered in the sticky remains of his lollipop. And in his arms, he cradled a bright red racing car.

"Jack!" Margit screamed joyfully. At the sound of his name, Jack stirred and opened his eyes. He smiled up at his sister and reached for her.

"Hi, Mah-git," he said drowsily. "I sleep. Car," he added, holding up the bright toy.

Mamma and Papa were by Margit's side in seconds. Mamma lunged for her son, squeezing him up to her face with such strength that Jack yelled to be let down.

"I don't know how we missed that spot," said a puzzled security guard, scratching his head. "These little fellas will find any nook or cranny to hide in. Well, I'm glad he's safe. And next time, Miss," he added, looking directly at Margit, "I suggest you hold on to your brother a little tighter."

Margit nodded and then she and her family left the store to go home.

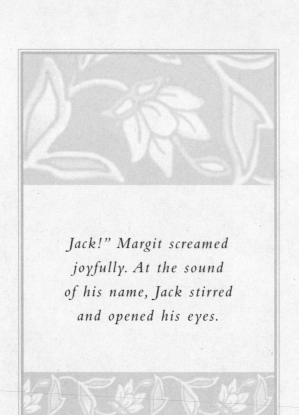

Jack!" Margit screamed
joyfully. At the sound
of his name, Jack stirred
and opened his eyes.

Margit and her parents barely spoke on the ride home. Alice was just as quiet and quickly said goodbye when her streetcar stop was called. Jack, however, chattered happily, still clutching his red racing car. The security guard had given it to him as a gift before they left the store. No one could have pried it from his hands, and no one wanted to try. Everyone was just relieved that things had turned out so well.

As soon as they entered the apartment, Margit disappeared into her room and slumped down on her bed. She was exhausted. Her body and her mind ached from the day's ordeal and she closed her eyes, desperately trying to forget everything that had happened. It was impossible. Once again, she had failed her parents—she'd let them down terribly. Margit was convinced that Mamma and Papa must truly hate her or be so supremely disappointed in her that they would never be able to forgive her. And Margit couldn't blame them. She *was* a failure. She wasn't worthy of their trust ever again. She had been crazy to think that her parents might be convinced to bring a Jewish orphan into their home. She couldn't even look after own her brother, let alone help with another child who was a stranger.

"I don't know how to tell you how sorry I am," Margit began as she and her parents sat down together, later that evening. Jack had been put to bed, still happily cradling his new car, oblivious to the fact that he had scared his parents and sister half out of their wits.

Papa sighed and rubbed his eyes. *Here it is,*

thought Margit. Her parents would finally tell her to her face that she was unreliable.

Papa began to talk, choosing his words carefully. "This was a hard day for all of us," he began. "We were so frightened. I can't remember feeling such fear since ..." Papa paused. Once again, Margit knew he was thinking about the war and the anguish he had felt when he was separated from his own family, not knowing when he would see them again. "But we're not blaming you, Margitka," Papa finally continued. "We know that you love Jack with all your heart, that you would never do anything that might harm him."

Margit could not believe what she was hearing. "But I was supposed to watch him every second and I didn't."

"Yes," continued Mamma. "It was a mistake to let go of him. But perhaps it was our mistake too. I let you go out with Jack for the whole day because I wanted a little time alone. Some days, it's hard enough watching Jack myself, let alone giving you that big job."

"But you trusted me, and I let you down."

Mamma smiled. "When you realized that it was an emergency, you did everything to find Jack that was possible. You searched with Alice, notified the security guards, and called your papa and me. You thought clearly and acted responsibly. We couldn't ask for more than that."

Margit sat back, blinking her eyes in astonishment. Her parents had not only forgiven her for today, but they were also actually trying to make her feel better about it—even taking some of the responsibility themselves.

"There's one thing more," added Papa.

Now it's coming, thought Margit. Finally, they were going to tell her about her punishment. This was what she had been expecting all along.

"We've thought so much about this, Margit," Papa continued. "But today, when we thought we had lost Jack, your mamma and I realized something. We couldn't begin to imagine our lives without him. We couldn't begin to imagine how this innocent child would feel to be without us, and you, Margit—the people who love him most." Papa paused and looked deeply into his daughter's eyes. "And so, Margit, we have decided that there is another child in this world who needs to have a family as well. We have decided that we will bring one of the orphans here to live with us."

Margit was too stunned to speak as Mamma continued talking. "That's right, Margit," said Mamma. "I kept thinking about you or Jack being all alone in the world. And that if that ever happened, all I would ever want is for another family to be there for you, to take care of you, and even to love you in our place. That's what we can do for one of these children."

Surely Margit had not heard correctly. Had her parents really just said that they were going to rescue one of the orphans? Mamma and Papa sat smiling at Margit, nodding their heads in unison.

"There is a lot that we will have to do," continued Mamma. "So much to prepare and think about. We will need all the help that you can give, Margit. Will you help make this happen?"

Still Margit could not speak. With her mouth wide open and her eyes shining brightly, Margit began to nod her head up and down with the energy and excitement that, moments before, had eluded her. Everything was fine once again. Everything would be wonderful from now on. A child was coming to live with them. A new chapter in her family's life was beginning.

CHAPTER N⁰ 11

The very next day, Papa contacted the Canadian Jewish Congress to tell them about the family's decision. The letter that arrived in response was courteous and warm:

We are delighted that you have decided to offer a home to one of the orphans. Your decision will make a difference in the lives of one of these unfortunate children. The children who will arrive in Canada are still recovering in hospitals across Europe and must be in good health to make the long journey overseas. We will keep you posted on their progress. In the meantime, we are grateful for your generosity and that of other families who have opened their hearts and homes.

"We don't know if the child will be a girl or a boy," said Mamma later that day as she sat mending a pair of Margit's old overalls. "But whatever this child doesn't use, we will give to the other children who come."

There was so much to do at home, and Margit and her family set to work, preparing for the eventual arrival of this child. Margit spent days rummaging through her drawers, pulling out sweaters that didn't fit and skirts that were too tight. Mamma could rework any article of clothing so that it would look like new. Books were next. Thoughtfully, Margit went through her bookshelf. *I know this child won't know any English. But eventually she ... or he will want to read something.* She pored over books like *Treasure Island, The Secret Garden, Anne of Green Gables,* and *The Adventures of Peter Rabbit. I guess I'll just have to choose a bit of everything,* Margit finally decided and set aside a pile of her books.

Jack was more reluctant to part with his toys. "This mine," he protested, as Mamma tried to gather some of his stuffed bears and old building blocks. Eventually Mamma had to wait until nighttime. Then, while Jack slept, she removed some old toys and placed them in a big box, away from where Jack could spot them. "I hope he won't recognize them when we pull them out for the child," said Mamma.

Even Alice got in on the preparations and arrived at Margit's apartment carrying blankets and a fluffy comforter from her family. "My mother thought you could use these," she said.

"Thank your mother for me, Alice," replied Mamma. "She is always so generous."

Alice and Margit disappeared into Margit's room. "I want to make some signs and banners," said Margit pointing to the art supplies on her desk. Alice nodded enthusiastically and the two girls set to work.

"We need a name," said Alice, holding up a sign with a colourful WELCOME printed in capital letters. "I can't just say 'Welcome, Boy' or 'Welcome, Girl.' That sounds so strange."

"I know," agreed Margit. "The Jewish Congress says we'll know who it is soon. Just say 'Welcome to Canada.' That's good enough for now." Alice nodded and the two girls continued working.

That night Margit had a dream that she was in the middle of a field surrounded by a group of children. They danced all around her, nameless boys and girls of different ages, waving at and beckoning to her. Margit reached out, trying to catch the hands of as many children as she could, and then she awoke with a start. It was hours before she could get back to sleep. There was something so exciting about not knowing who this child would be, almost like the pleasure of a birthday surprise. But it was also beginning to feel scary. A stranger was about to enter her life. What if this child didn't like her and didn't want to live with Margit's family?

One day, Papa arrived home behind the wheel of an old pickup truck. "Mr. Hillock let me use his truck so I could bring this home," he said, unlatching the back panel. "It's a couch that opens to a bed. When I told Mr. Hillock about the child, he told me to take it, said his family was planning to get a new chesterfield anyway."

"He is so kind," Mamma cried.

"He said it's old but comfortable."

Mamma and Papa struggled to lift the sofa off the back of the truck. Margit pushed from behind, and somehow the three of them managed to lug the couch up the narrow stairs and into the apartment.

"It's perfect," said Mamma. "I have a pretty blanket we can put on top to hide these fraying arms. No one will see."

The next morning, Margit was busy getting ready for school when there was a knock at the door.

"Ask who it is before you open," called Mamma from the kitchen. "And watch that Jack doesn't run out."

Margit lunged after her brother and called through the door. "Who's there, please?"

"Special delivery letter. I'll need a signature."

Margit opened the door as Papa appeared, adjusting his tie. He accepted the letter, signed his name, and closed the door. "It's from the Canadian Jewish Congress," said Papa turning the letter over in his hands.

"Open it, Papa. Quick!" Margit shouted, impatiently.

Papa ran his thumb under the seal and tore open the flap. He reached inside and pulled out a single sheet of paper, reading it quickly. Then he looked into the envelope once more and smiled.

"It will be a girl," he said, taking out a faded black-and-white photograph and holding it up. "Nine years old. Her name is Lilly."

CHAPTER Nᵒ 12

*Margit stared at the photograph, mesmer-*ized by the face of the young girl who stared back at her. "Lilly." She repeated the name over and over, as if the girl in the picture might answer if she heard her name being called. It's a girl. She is nine years old. Her name is Lilly.

Margit had been waiting for this moment, but instead of feeling excited, she was suddenly terrified. *What have I done?* she wondered as she stared intently at the photo and into Lilly's sad eyes. *I finally know your name, but I don't know anything about who you are.*

"The information says that she is from Poland," continued Papa. "I imagine she knows no English. It will be a challenge trying to talk with this little Polish girl. But I remember what it was like to learn a new language. So, she'll learn, just as we did."

"This is wonderful!" cried Mamma. "Imagine, Margit. This little girl is coming to our home. Now that we know who she is, we really have so much to do." She chattered on, seemingly unaware of Margit's hesitation. "When will the child arrive, Leo? Does the letter say?"

Papa scanned through the letter and nodded. "Yes, yes, here it is. One month from now, in July. A boat will arrive in Halifax Harbour, carrying the first group of orphans. From there, they will travel by trains to cities across the country. Wait, there's more," he said as he continued reading. "Listen to this. We are invited to go to Halifax for the arrival of the boat and to meet Lilly."

Mamma gasped as Papa looked up. "Halifax," she repeated. "Do you remember, Margit? Just like when we arrived two years ago."

How could Margit forget? The memory of her arrival in Canada was fixed in her mind. She could picture the sight of the approaching land from the ship, imagine the immigration officials and their endless questions, and hear the sound of English being spoken for the first time. But most of all, she could remember the fear. And that was only the beginning. The real journey began after she had arrived: learning to live in this country. At least Margit had had her mother with her every step of the way. Now Lilly was making that same difficult passage all by herself.

"I think one of us should go," continued Mamma, as if she had read Margit's mind. "It will be so much easier if we meet the child there. It's hard enough that she has travelled alone from Europe. I don't want her to be alone on the train to Toronto."

Papa nodded. "You're right, Miriam. I'll speak to Mr. Hillock. I'm certain he'll agree to give me a few days off. It would be impossible for you to leave Jack behind or to take him with you. I'll go and bring the child here."

"And me," interrupted Margit. "Take me, Papa." Her mother and father stared back at her. "It will be summer vacation. I won't miss school. Besides, I'm the one who started this whole thing. I need to meet her. I need to go with you." Margit was still uncertain about this whole venture and about everything that the coming months would bring. But she knew in her heart that she had to be the one who met Lilly first, who faced her and brought her to her family's home.

Papa was the first to break the silence. "Yes," he agreed, nodding at his daughter. "We'll go together, Margit."

CHAPTER N⁰ 13

And so, one month later, Margit found herself standing in the immigration building by the pier in Halifax, next to her father. Surrounding them were members of the Jewish Congress, officials from the City of Halifax, men and women from the community, newspaper reporters, and photographers, all waiting to catch a first glimpse of the newcomers. Margit stood on her tiptoes, stretching her neck to see above the crowd. *Which one is she?* wondered Margit, staring at the group of young boys and girls neatly lined up at the immigration counters.

Their expressions, even from this distance, were painful; large hollow eyes staring suspiciously from pale faces. Margit felt a knot in her own stomach. It twisted so tightly that, for a moment, she worried she might be sick. Papa placed a reassuring hand on his daughter's shoulder.

"Come," he said. "Let's meet Lilly."

And suddenly, there she was, standing in front of Margit and her father. The immigration official was saying something to Papa, showing him papers and explaining where he had to sign to take charge of Lilly. It was just like she was a package being delivered into their hands. "Sign here and here, and then we're all done," the man said, tipping his hat and walking away. Margit barely heard a thing. She stared wordlessly at the young girl in front of her.

The same sad eyes that had stared at her from the black-and-white photograph now stared back at her in the large hall. Lilly's deep brown eyes held a painful past that Margit could not understand. Lilly reached up to adjust the faded grey ribbon that held her straight brown hair in place. She shuddered slightly. Was it the morning dampness, lack of sleep, or fear that made her shiver? She shifted her small, square-cornered suitcase from one hand to the other nervously. Papa immediately reached for the suitcase but Lilly would not let go. She held on tightly, afraid to hand it over, afraid perhaps that she would not get it back. But Papa nodded calmly and eventually Lilly surrendered the case.

Margit glanced down at the brown tag pinned to Lilly's faded green coat. It said "ORPHAN" and then "CN 25." The CN stood for Canadian National Railway and 25 was Lilly's identification number. It was as if she herself had been tagged like a piece of luggage.

"Hello," Margit finally said, reaching out to shake hands with Lilly.

"Goodbye," Lilly replied in a tiny voice. Margit stifled a laugh. Lilly seemed to know that these were greetings, but she had no idea that one was for coming and the other for going.

"How are you?" Margit continued, trying to make a connection with this young girl.

"How are you?" Lilly repeated slowly and with a thick accent.

Margit sighed. This was going to be tough, but she would not give up. She reached behind her back, into a bag that she had brought with her from home, and pulled out a large doll. In the weeks leading up to Lilly's arrival, Margit had pooled together all her money. She had gone back to the Eaton's store and to the toy department to buy this doll, which she had seen with Alice only a few months earlier—the doll named Violet. Margit looked down at its dark eyes and hair and its pale face. Except for its beautiful lace dress, it almost looked like Lilly with her sad expression.

Margit held the doll out to Lilly and waited. Slowly Lilly reached out and took the doll in her arms, cradling it against her chest and cheek. She gazed back at Margit and a tiny smile began to creep across her face. After the briefest moment,

"Hello," Margit finally said,
reaching out to shake
hands with Lilly.
"Goodbye," Lilly replied
in a tiny voice.

it was gone, as if Lilly were afraid to smile or had forgotten how to.

But for Margit it was something, a beginning, and that was good enough for now. She reached out and removed the tag that was pinned to Lilly's coat.

"Come on," Margit said to her father. "Let's take Lilly home."

Papa nodded and turned around, carrying Lilly's bag. Margit paused and reached her hand out once more to Lilly. There was a long moment of silence. Lilly stared at Margit. Then, she lifted her arm and slipped her hand into Margit's. Holding hands, the two girls turned and followed Papa out the door.

AUTHOR'S NOTE

There are several references to real documents in this story.

CHAPTER 1

The letter that Charity Grant reads at the synagogue is one she wrote to Brooke Claxton, Minister of Health and Welfare, on January 20, 1946 (Source: Canadian Jewish Congress Archives).

CHAPTER 5

The headlines that Margit finds in the newspaper are from the *Victoria Daily Times,* Saturday, May 3, 1947.

CHAPTER 7

The article that Margit reads to her parents comes from a bulletin published by the Canadian Jewish Congress (Source: National Archives).

CHAPTER 9

The opening lines of *Kathie's Three Wishes* by Amanda M. Douglas (Boston: Lee and Shepard, 1881) appear as they were published in the book.

Acknowledgements

My thanks to Barbara Berson, Eliza Marciniak, Dawn Hunter, and all those at Penguin Group (Canada) for their dedication to this project. It is an honour to be a part of the Our Canadian Girl series. My love as always to my friends and family, especially my husband, Ian Epstein, and my children, Gabi and Jake.

Dear Reader,

*Welcome back to Our Canadian Girl!
In addition to this story about Margit,
there are many more adventures of other
spirited girls to come.*

*So please keep on reading. And do stay
in touch. You can also log on to our website
at www.ourcanadiangirl.ca and enjoy fun
activities, sample chapters, a fan club, and
monthly contests.*

*Sincerely,
Barbara Berson
Editor*

1608
Samuel de Champlain establishes the first fortified trading post at Quebec.

1759
The British defeat the French in the Battle of the Plains of Abraham.

1812
The United States declares war against Canada.

1845
The expedition of Sir John Franklin to the Arctic ends when the ship is frozen in the pack ice; the fate of its crew remains a mystery.

1869
Louis Riel leads his Métis followers in the Red River Rebellion.

1871
British Columbia joins Canada.

1755
The British expel the entire French population of Acadia (today's Maritime provinces), sending them into exile.

1776
The 13 Colonies revolt against Britain, and the Loyalists flee to Canada.

1837
Calling for responsible government, the Patriotes, following Louis-Joseph Papineau, rebel in Lower Canada; William Lyon Mackenzie leads the uprising in Upper Canada.

1867
New Brunswick, Nova Scotia and the United Province of Canada come together in Confederation to form the Dominion of Canada.

1870
Manitoba joins Canada. The Northwest Territories become an official territory of Canada.

1762
Elizabeth

1862
Lisa

Timeline

1885
At Craigellachie, British Columbia, the last spike is driven to complete the building of the Canadian Pacific Railway.

1898
The Yukon Territory becomes an official territory of Canada.

1914
Britain declares war on Germany, and Canada, because of its ties to Britain, is at war too.

1918
As a result of the Wartime Elections Act, the women of Canada are given the right to vote in federal elections.

1945
World War II ends conclusively with the dropping of atomic bombs on Hiroshima and Nagasaki.

1873
Prince Edward Island joins Canada.

1896
Gold is discovered on Bonanza Creek, a tributary of the Klondike River.

1905
Alberta and Saskatchewan join Canada.

1917
In the Halifax harbour, two ships collide, causing an explosion that leaves more than 1,600 dead and 9,000 injured.

1939
Canada declares war on Germany seven days after war is declared by Britain and France.

1949
Newfoundland, under the leadership of Joey Smallwood, joins Canada.

1897
Emily

1948
Margit

Read more about Margit
in Book One:
Home Free

Fleeing war-torn Czechoslovakia in 1944, Margit discovers a new world of freedom in Toronto.

Find out what happens when Margit's
father comes home from the war
in Book Two:

A Bit of Luck and A Bit of Love

Margit's family is whole again—but life in
Canada is not as perfect as she had hoped.
Her father is struggling to find work,
and Margit starts to fail at school.
How can she tell her parents?

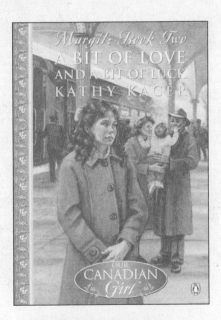